My sister and I first heard the story of Clever Tortoise when we were small. We lived in East Africa then, in Tanzania. We thought it was a new story (because _we_ had just heard it), but it was an old story that the Ngoni people of southern Tanzania would tell each other.

Making this book of it, all this time later, the bush came flooding back to me — its different lights and smells, the animals and insects, the colours of lake water, the ground that is so interesting when you have only little legs.

I have put some Kiswahili words into this version of the story. I hope you will not find them hard. It is the language most widely spoken in Tanzania. The sound of it in my ears makes me remember other sounds of East Africa — like storm rain drumming, cicadas singing, and the noise of two little girls laughing over the clever trick that Clever Tortoise played on the banks of Lake Nyasa. I hope you will laugh too...

NYOKA
snake

CHUNGU
black ant

CLEVER TORTOISE

A traditional African tale

Francesca Martin

WALKER BOOKS
AND SUBSIDIARIES
LONDON · BOSTON · SYDNEY

NYUKI
bee

NGIRI
warthog

KISUNGURA
rabbit

KOBE
tortoise

PANYA
rat

MJUSI
lizard

CHURA
frog

Listen!
There is a lake in Africa, called Nyasa.
Mmm, it is full of blue cool water.

On the banks of Nyasa live
Rabbit, Warthog, Lizard,
Hippopotamus, Snake, Elephant,
Chungu – the little black ant –
and many other animals.

Clever Tortoise lives there too.

See? Everyone is happy now.
But once there was a quarrel.
Hm, tch, tch, it started like this...

"See how big I am?"
cried Elephant one day.
"I am stronger than all you
little animals!"

And a great big
elephant-sized crashing
and trampling
and spoiling
and stamping
began in the bush by Lake Nyasa.

Ooh, tch, tch, it was bad.

Hm, and it was catching.

"See how huge I am?" cried Hippopotamus another day. "I am stronger than all you small animals!"

And a great huge hippopotamus-sized splashing and bubbling and churning started in the waters of Lake Nyasa.

Aah, tch, tch! It was worse.

Rabbit, Snake, Lizard and the others grew frightened.

Warthog called a meeting.
"What shall we do?" he said.
"That Elephant and that Hippopotamus are bullies."

All the animals thought.

Clever Tortoise thought too.
Ahh! that tortoise. His head is small, but his brains are big and strong.
"Ha!" he said, after just a little time.
"Let's play a trick on them..."

Pitter-patter, pitter-patter.
Clever Tortoise led the others
through the bush to find Elephant.

"Mr Mighty Elephant," Clever Tortoise
called. "I hear you are the strongest.
Will you fight a tug-of-war with me?"

"You?" snorted Elephant.
"A little teeny tortoise?
Fight a tug-of-war with ME!"

"Yes," said Clever Tortoise. "I will
meet you right here at sun-up
tomorrow, with a rope."

Pitter-patter, pitter-patter.
Then Clever Tortoise took the others
to the water to find Hippopotamus.

"Mrs Fine Hippopotamus," Clever
Tortoise said. "I hear you are the strongest.
Will you fight a tug-of-war with me?"

"You?" scoffed Hippopotamus.
"A weeny small tortoise?
Fight a tug-of-war with ME!"

"Yes," said Clever Tortoise. "I will meet
you right here at sun-up tomorrow,
with a rope."

That night, Clever Tortoise,
Rabbit, Warthog, Lizard and
the others stayed awake.

My! What rustling and tying,
what rolling and twisting,
what knotting and plaiting
of long strong tree vines there was –
all through star-time.

To weave one long strong rope.

Ha!

The sun rose,
and the blue cool water
of Lake Nyasa
turned to red and gold.

Elephant rose too.

"Good morning, Mr Elephant,"
Clever Tortoise said. "Will you
take this end of our tug-of-war
rope? Then we can begin."

"Huh!" snorted Elephant.
"I will pull you over quicker than
a hummingbird beats its wings!"

But where do you think
Clever Tortoise and his friends
went with the *other* end of their
long strong rope?

Ha!

"Good morning, Mrs Hippopotamus,"
Clever Tortoise said. "Will you take
this end of our tug-of-war rope?
Then we can begin."

"Humph!" snorted Hippopotamus.
"I will pull you over faster
than a frog can jump!"

But that boasty Hippopotamus
and that proud Elephant,
they had one enormous surprise
coming their way...

"NGGHHHHH!"
grunted Elephant.
"MMMMMPH!"
groaned Hippopotamus,
as the tug-of-war began.

"OOOOOOOF!"
moaned Elephant.
"AI-AI!" gasped
Hippopotamus,
as the tug-of-war went on.

And each of them thought,
"This tincy tortoise,
he is very strangely
STRONG."

The sun climbed high
and higher in the sky,
till there was not one
shadow left in all Africa.
Ooh, and it was hot.

But still the rope stayed tight.

"Enough!" said Clever Tortoise.
And he cut the rope
with a little stone axe.

Well, what do you think
happened then?

CRASH! fell Elephant,
and he bumped his big strong head.

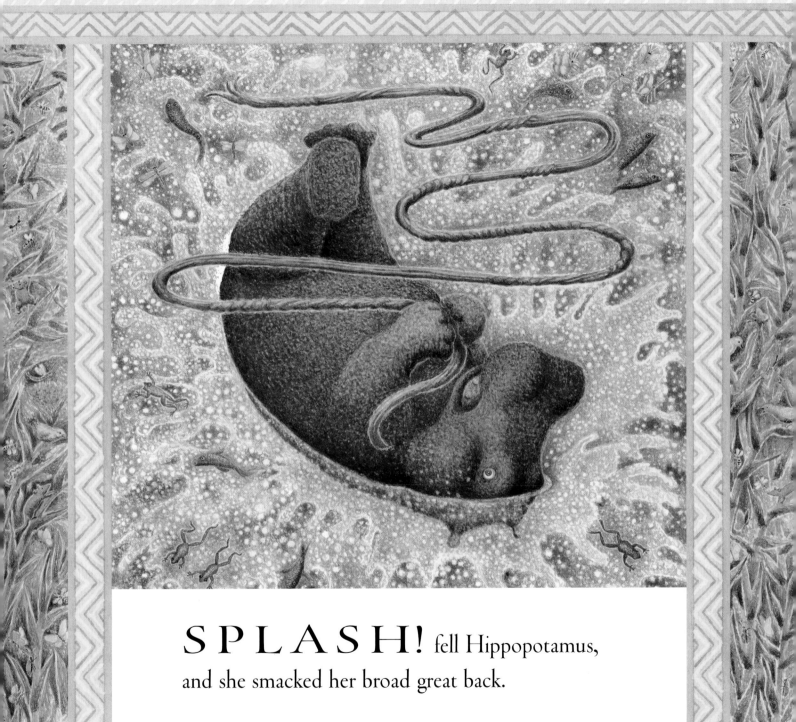

SPLASH! fell Hippopotamus,
and she smacked her broad great back.

Pitter-patter, pitter-patter.

Clever Tortoise went to visit Elephant in the bush.

"'Quicker than a hummingbird beats its wings'?" he called.

Elephant just stared at that teeny tortoise.

Where did he hide his strength? In his toes?

Pitter-patter, pitter-patter.

Clever Tortoise went to visit Hippopotamus by the water.

"'Faster than a frog can jump'?" he called.

Hippopotamus just gazed at that weeny tortoise.

Where did he hide his strength? Underneath his shell?

That night, Elephant and
Hippopotamus slept a deep
tired tug-of-war sleep.
But the smaller animals stayed awake.

My! What clapping and swinging,
what dancing and jumping
happened in the moonlight!

"You clever Clever Tortoise!" cheered
Rabbit, Warthog, Lizard, Snake,
Chungu – the little black ant – and all
the others. "That was one good trick!"

And that's how that quarrel was mended.

See? All the animals are happy again.

Kwa heri ya kuonana, wanangu –
so long, children, till we meet again.

For my sister, Philly

I would like to thank Helen Read for
the decorative borders she has designed and
painted so beautifully, and Lucy Ingrams,
whose ideas have brought rhythm and
humour to the text.

First published 2000 by Walker Books Ltd
87 Vauxhall Walk, London SE11 5HJ

2 4 6 8 10 9 7 5 3 1

© 2000 Francesca Martin

This book has been typeset in ThrohandInk.

Printed in Hong Kong

British Library Cataloguing in Publication Data
A catalogue record for this book is
available from the British Library.

ISBN 0-7445-5518-3